Cosmic Cat
and the Pink Planet

by Colin and Jacqui Hawkins

LIONS

To Sally and Finbar

First published in Great Britain 1988 by Picture Lions
Picture Lions is an imprint of the Children's Division
of Collins Publishing Group, 8, Grafton St, London W1X 3LA

Copyright © Colin Hawkins 1988

ISBN 0 00 662736-6

Printed and bound in Great Britain by
William Collins Sons & Co. Ltd, Glasgow

THE COSMIC CREW

COSMIC CAT

Captain and top cat
aboard the S.S. Sherbert

PADDY O'TABBY

chief engineer and
D.I.Y. enthusiast

KITTY

First Officer
and medic

HOGS

Star navigator
and cook.

... and
introducing

DAARG,
a jungle hero.

In the darkest depths of deep space Cosmic Cat and his crew are under attack. It is their dreaded enemy the savage and ferocious... **KURS!**

They're closing in fast, Captain!

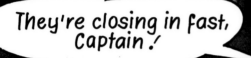

Zap!

Zap!

Z

The Kur battle cruiser thunders closer and closer firing its lethal laser bolts. The Cosmic crew are in trouble!

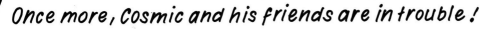

The Cosmic crew are prisoners of the Goofs—a wild and hairy race of woollie bullies that inhabit the dense jungle.

The Goofs poke and prod their captives through the jungle towards a gigantic pink statue.

Hundreds of Goots crowd round the prisoners. Their huge jaws chatter excitedly... 'Greet... Greet!' (Gootish for 'GREAT... GREAT!')

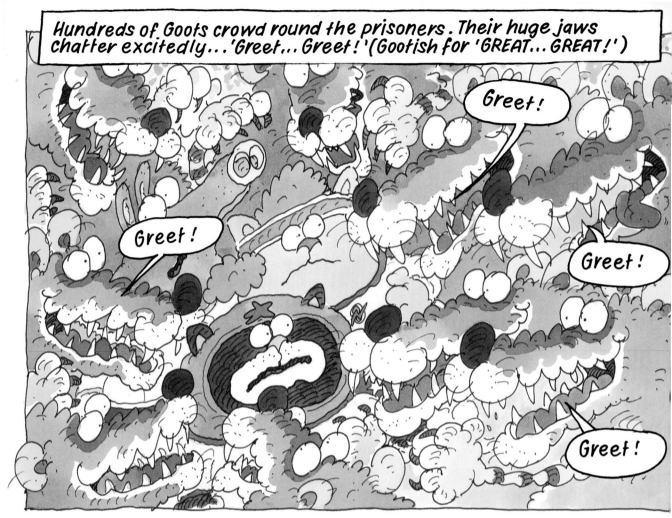

Greet!

Greet!

Greet!

Greet!

BEEP! BEEP! BEEP!

Suddenly the scanner on Hog's wrist bleeps urgently.

BEEP! BEEP!

Cummon!

At the bottom of a deep pit are hundreds of wriggling, hissing snakes. They have sharp, deadly poisonous teeth!

With the vital Katonium the hyperdrive can function once again. The Cosmic heroes are ready for more adventures through time and space.

Me space Daarg now !